4th Birthday
To: Jaden
From: Aunt Deb &
    Uncle Bruce

We hope you enjoy
this story & have
a wonderful time
on your 4th Birthday!

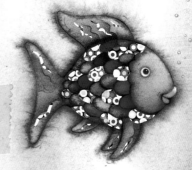

This book is for:

Jade

From: Aunt Deb
& uncle
Bruise

The illustrations in this book have appeared previously in
The Rainbow Fish
Rainbow Fish to the Rescue
Rainbow Fish and the Big Blue Whale
Rainbow Fish and the Sea Monster's Cave
Rainbow Fish Finds His Way

First published in the United States and Canada in 2008 by NorthSouth Books,
an imprint of NordSüd Verlag AG, Zürich, Switzerland.
Distributed in the United States by NorthSouth Books Inc., New York.

Library of Congress Cataloging-in-Publication Data is available.
ISBN 13: 978-0-7358-2200-9 (trade edition).
Printed in China
1 3 5 7 9 10 8 6 4 2

For more information about our books and the authors and artists
who create them, visit our web site: www.northsouth.com.

Marcus Pfister

A GIFT FROM THE
Rainbow Fish

NORTHSOUTH
BOOKS

There are lots of ways to share.
Sometimes it's easy.
Sometimes it's hard.
But when you share with your friends,
they will share with you too.

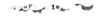

I am the Rainbow Fish.
Once I had many sparkly scales.
No one else had scales as pretty as mine.
When I shared my scales,
I made lots of friends.
Now we swim together and make the ocean sparkle.

Sometimes the ocean is dangerous.
Once I shared my hiding place
with a little striped fish.
Then we were *both* safe.
If I am in trouble someday,
I know he will share his safest place with me.

When I am frightened,
I hurry to find my friends.
When we are together,
things don't seem as scary.

When I don't know what to do,
I ask the wise octopus.
I share my problem.
He shares his advice.

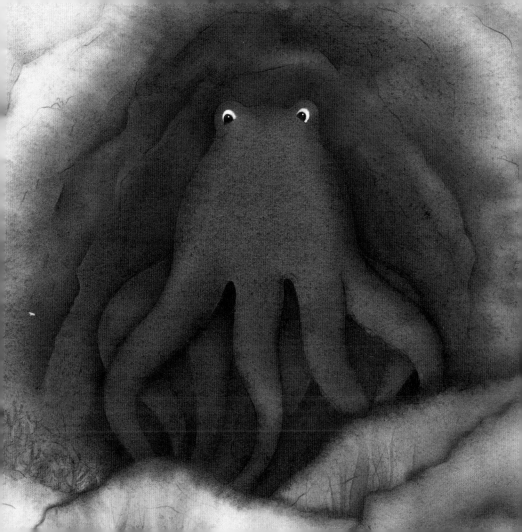

My friend the whale is always hungry,
but he shares his food with us.
There is enough for all, he says.

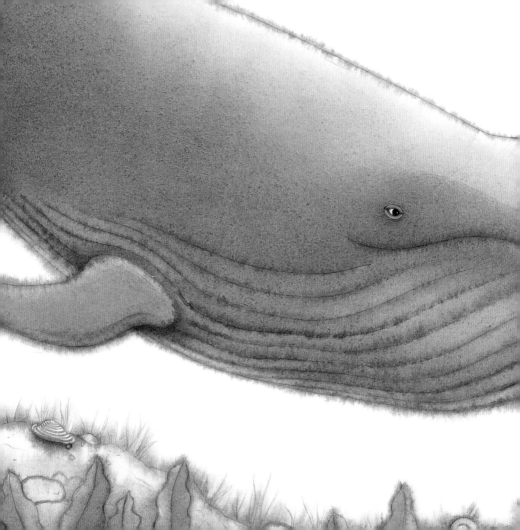

I share my secrets with the whale.
We are friends.
We trust each other.

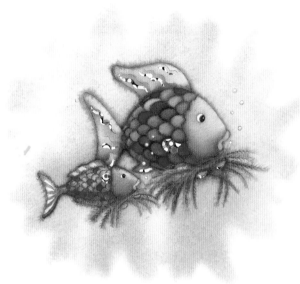

This load of seaweed was too heavy
for the little blue fish.
It was too heavy for me too,
so we shared the load.
Sharing the work makes it easier.

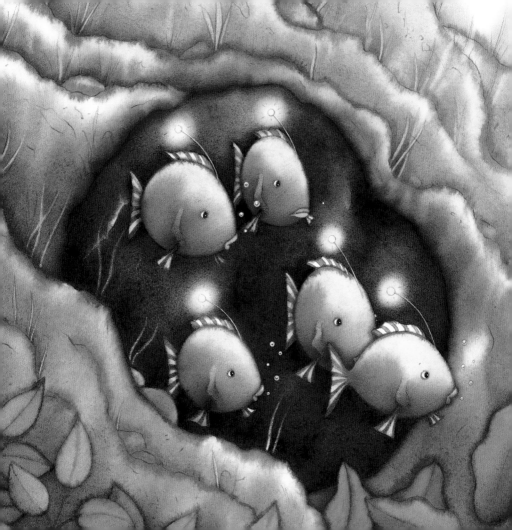

We didn't have to swim home in the dark.
The lantern fish lit our way.
They shared their lights with us.

I have something I'd like to share with you.